Frog

Huggums

Bun Bun

Little Sister

Gator

Bat Child

Maurice & Molly

Oscar

BAT CHILD'S
HAUNTED HOUSE

BY MERCER MAYER

RANDOM HOUSE 🏠 NEW YORK

BAT CHILD'S HAUNTED HOUSE

BY MERCER MAYER

Bat Child lived in a snug little cave
under a hill.

One day, Malcom came by.

"If you were a brave bat, you would live in a haunted house," Malcom said.

Bat Child wanted to be a brave bat,
so he set off to find a haunted house.
"We'll miss you," said his friends.

Finally, on top of
a windy hill,
Bat Child found
what looked like
a haunted house.

Bat Child went to the attic of the haunted house,
but the attic was already full of bats.
"There's no more room," said the bats.

Bat Child went to
the basement, but a
mouse family lived there.
"You can't live here,"
said the mice.

BLESS THIS
HOUSE
KEEP US FAT
AND SAVE
US FROM THE
PUSSY
CAT

The closets were full of ghosts!
"Come in," said the ghosts. "We don't
take up much room. You may stay with us."

Meanwhile, Malcom thought he
would scare Bat Child.
He put on a sheet. Then he
stood outside the haunted house
and made a racket.

From that moment on, Bat Child knew that he was a brave bat and that Malcom was a scaredy-cat.

So Bat Child flew home to his snug little cave under a hill.

Bat Child's friends had a welcome home party
just for him.
"You don't have to live in a haunted house
to be a brave bat," everyone shouted.

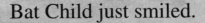

Bat Child just smiled.

He already knew that.

Possum Child

Mouse

Max

Seaweed

Little Critter

Skat Owl

Mooso

Malcom